The Heal

The Healer's Code

Iba Malik

Published by Iba Malik, 2023.

I dedicate this work to all those who have supported me throughout my journey.

To my family, who has been my constant source of love and encouragement. Your unwavering support has given me the strength to pursue my dreams and overcome any challenges that came my way.

To my friends, who have been there for me in both good times and bad. Your friendship has brought joy, laughter, and comfort to my life, and I am grateful for each and every one of you.

To my teachers, who have shared their knowledge and wisdom with me. Your guidance and expertise have shaped my understanding and helped me grow both personally and professionally.

To all the readers reading my book, who have shown interest and appreciation for my ideas and efforts. Your engagement has motivated me to continue exploring and sharing my thoughts. Thank you for the audience reading this book.

Lastly, I would like to dedicate this work to myself, as a reminder of the perseverance and determination that brought me to this point. May this dedication serve as a testimony to the countless hours of hard work, sacrifices, and passion that went into creating this piece. Thank you all for being a part of my journey. This work is dedicated to each and every one of you.

Foreword

It was a simple thought that had begun my journey of writing, I previously had thought of the same characters and a similar plot but instead the setting to be outer space. But I had thought that it would interest readers if it was just on land instead of an intergalactic journey where a pandemic occurs, the reason being that it is highly unlikely for a disease to start in space, according to the storyline, so, I decided to start this idea.

The grumpy character of Sally Harriet is extremely iconic to me. A character that is depicted as dreary, sullen and menacing begins to understand life and its importance of surroundings and ends up being altruistic, compassionate, generous and cheery. Likewise, at the end what happens to her is a sort of shock but also sparks kindness in her cold soul and heart, which now also can be indirectly shown as a morality tale.

This story that I made is supposed to have a meaning. Either a significant lesson that is weaved and woven whilst writing a story, or a lesson that can be taught at the end, either way, writing a story with a major meaning comes to be a challenge and not all can accomplish, but one thing is for sure, anyone can write a story because anyone can be an author, there is no criteria and specific ideas for a person to become a writer, I believe anyone can, it just is really challenging to complete it.

This book is packed with pleasing memories. It took me eight months of hard work to make my dream of writing come true. The excitement surrounding its release was truly amazing, especially because my about-to-be readers were eagerly waiting for it.

Thank you for reading this and I really do hope that my book can teach people, especially young people, that anybody can be an author and that it doesn't matter of age, as age is just a number.

Iba Malik

May 2023

Prologue

In the corners of a hospital, a single vial teetered on the edge of a pristine white countertop, made by people who wanted to spill their cruelty towards everyone, attempting to destroy mass civilians. Little did the world know, within its delicate glass walls, a secret so terrifying and unpredictable was about to unravel, and someone had to stop it before the tea would spill. A sombre and unassuming lady, cloaked in misery and shrouded from the notice of others, embarked upon a difficult quest to unearth a remedy with her fellow colleagues. Though drained and affected by irritability, her resolve remained firm, driven solely by a ravenous desire for universal bliss and solid security.

Yet was it not strange? A lady gripped by a maelstrom of anger and hopelessness, yet absurdly yearning for the flourishing of her surroundings. Her heart had very little compassion but would oddly weep silently at the passing of every fellow citizen ensnared by the malevolent malady. Despite the curtain of her attitude, a hidden pool of kindness coursed through her being, dedicated and firm in her pursuit of charity.

If you showed resilience, wouldn't you achieve your goal? A lady so once enthralled by fury was now one of the gentlest of all, showing charity nearly every day, a twinkling glimmer in her eye when arousing from her deep slumber. If you showed joy, wouldn't you achieve your target? Yes, now that she has found what's desired to be found, she could prosper and become joyous. If you showed endurance and caution, wouldn't you achieve your goal? Yes, because patience is a virtue and care for, care for yourself before others but the lady took it as a gift this quote and has tended for it since then.

Achieve your goal through happiness, care, resilience and patience and see that is guaranteed you will prosper.

Chapter 1 – The Dream Is Interrupted

A loud yell from outside of the house awakened the relaxed lady, the lady was stunned and was grumbling as she tossed and turned, eager to get that dream back.

The dream was that she was flying, with gorgeous plumose wings, soaring through the sky with a trace of glittering rainbows after her, there were eagles and birds airborne with her, squealing and screeching, their cotton-like ends bobbling up and down as they moved efficiently.

But clearly, every day, she would be bothered by that yell, the shout that could be considered as her alarm clock.

She scrambled into her PPE clothes, brushed her hair and did her daily things, she hurried out with a frown, her eyes were slightly red by the lack of sleep, it was only in sleep did she think she was ever content.

"Dr. Harriet, good to see you slightly...um...calm." The man said, it was Dr. Carter (John Carter) who was hollering in the morning, he was also a medic, like Sally Harriet, he was a jolly and positive man, but was lately worried by the current disease increasing across the town, it was called 'Deathbell Disease'.

"Yes, *definitely* calm. I'm *definitely* not frustrated by your daily racket, not to mention the loud screams of those inane children frolicking around like clowns." Sally articulated, in a 'calm' voice, she grinned sardonically, and spun around to indicate the kids.

"Sally, please, they're just youngsters. Anyways that's not the problem, it's about the Deathbell Disease epidemic!" John said, he gripped onto a notepad, the pad was written all about the symptoms of the Deathbell disease.

"You think I have enough energy...ah forget it. You've been bringing up this situation so many times, why is it such a popular issue?" Sally mumbled crossly, sighing as John explained for at least 15 minutes. They were walking swiftly to the medical centre as they spoke.

"It's serious, Sally. A number of people in the town have died, and even Dr. Uriah Raymond died as well." John bowed his head in anguish, Sally narrowed her eyes.

"Really, Raymond wasn't even nice." Sally murmured darkly, though her voice was loud, and all the medics glanced at her, their eyes broadened.

"Sally! Your awfully insolent, you know! Just because you didn't like Uriah, doesn't mean he was a wicked man. He crafted the Core Vial, the essence that assisted fish with rabies." Alicia yelled, she was clasping onto a vial and inspected it with her hands, as if it was some new machinery.

"Yeah, Uriah is a *legend*." A lady said, beaming, and putting her hands on her hips.

"Anyhow, come with me." John told Sally to put goggles and more gear on, then he led her into the medical room, where dozens of citizens were vomiting and choking by the disease. Some were resting on the beds, shuddering, struggling to breathe.

Sally held her breath.

"You see what I'm trying to say. It's urgent, Sally. The citizens and their families are relying on *us* to protect them from this horrid virus, we *need* every specialist and every person in the medical field to assist us. We are the only high-standard hospital in the country, people are travelling from other cities just to get a few hours of treatment! Think that!" John exclaimed as he shook his head and strode on.

Sally thought that this was terrifying. That she wasn't ready to combat this new burst. It was so abrupt, so unexpected, that it wreaked chaos in minutes when the news had dispersed.

She followed John, her head lowered in grief, her mind revolving around her thoughts.

It was lunch time when she made her way to the refectory, she was sat on a chair, silent, chomping on her food, still thinking.

"Can Dr. Sally Harriet please arrive to the Deputy Doctor's Office?" The announcement articulated; its loud voice echoed in the canteen.

Everybody eyed Sally, who flushed in awkwardness, her heart was beating rapidly, everyone knew that if someone had to go to the DDO (Deputy Doctor's Office) it probably meant something bad.

She got up from her chair, placed the empty tray on the counter, and tottered out, her legs were wobbly, she felt jittery, everybody watched her leave and cringed as the enormous oak doors screeched.

She knocked on the office door, waited, and listened to the footsteps, the noise of somebody arranging paper, and then the door creaked open.

"Come in!" A feverish voice shrieked, Sally bounded and walked in.

"Ahh...if it isn't Sally who I called from 10-15 minutes ago. Why so late, Sally Harriet?" A lady in rubicund heels alleged, she wore a lengthy and stylish white dress covered in printed green plants and rosy blossoms, she was sitting on a chair behind a timber desk. The lady had glossy jet-black hair, had emerald green eyes, she was strict, her eyes flashed in fury.

"Sorry, Miss...." Sally murmured, she didn't know the lady's name, Sally stared at her blankly.

"Juanita is my name; you can call me Juana if you want. You are Sally Harriet, ah...the daughter of your *madre* who has supposed to also be one of my best doctors, Maria Harriet." Juana miserably gazed down in sorrow, her mood and tone of voice had altered, she had known Sally's mother had died of a malignant illness, which had really impacted Sally. "Don't be gloomy." Juana murmured, Sally nodded miserably, Juana's expressions were alleviated with compassion and sympathy.

"Anyways, I need you to visit the reception to obtain an envelope. Do that and come back swiftly." Juana articulated, she told Sally to leave, and Sally hurried out of the door with her sullen expression.

She didn't know a teensy person was following her.

Chapter 2 – Tiny People

Sally was walking back to the office, her hands gripping the envelope, when she felt a touch on her back. She spun around, and gasped, she backed away, it was a little girl.

"Hi! Hi! Are you a doctor? A nurse? What are you?!" The little girl cried in glee, she dashed to Sally, who was running to the office, for some reason, terrified.

"A child, Sally thought, *who the hell brought a child?! Why is she chasing me and asking me stuff?"*

The little girl was asking random questions, some about medical stuff, some extremely...silly.

"Do doctors ride magic flying ponies when there is danger? Can magical ponies help sick people? Are unicorns real?" The girl was chasing her, asking all those questions that Sally thought was awfully stupid.

"I have to stop...goodness me..." Sally turned to the girl; the girl innocently stared at her with cerulean eyes.

"W-what do you want?" Sally questioned, slightly irate.

The little girl said nothing, there was a lurid cough from the sickbay room where the ill people were resting, the girl squealed and clutched behind Sally onto her PPE clothes. Sally did nothing, it was a typical noise.

"Why are you frightened? Get off!" Sally brushed the clutching small hand of the girl, the girl put her hands on her side and stared back.

"What do you-, ugh.... come with me. And no holding hands, no hugs, no idiotic behaviour. Understood?" Sally said commandingly, the girl watched back, nodded and danced.

"I said no idiotic behaviour!" Sally shouted at the girl, who stopped abruptly.

Sally took the little girl to the office, whilst listening to the soft hum of a nursery rhyme from the girl. She groaned and grumbled as she knocked on the door.

Sally entered the room, smiling timidly at Juana, who gaped back in shock.

"What is that girl doing here? Sally? Care to explain? I swear, if you don't have a good excuse you will be fired!" Juana had a smug face, the little girl stared at Sally, in which Sally laughed fretfully.

Swiftly, A flash of pink light blinded Sally, she heard a loud scream, was its Juana's?

She woke up, still standing, her head resting on the walls, she gazed beside her, the little girl was standing, scared, the girl looked pale.

Juana was dead on the floor.

"WHAT?! What have you done?!" Sally glanced at her with a terrified face, the little girl looked back and said nothing. Sally backed away from her, scared and paranoid, it couldn't be that the little girl had murdered Juana?

No. That can't be right.

"I have not done anything! I saw, bad thing, lady was coughing, she *dead.*" The little girl was pointing at Juana, who was lying lifeless on the floor.

Sally was still breathing fast, when she had fainted on the spot.

Sally awoke, alarmed, her breath still fast, she was lying on the hospital beds, thankfully not in the sickbay, but a private room, with a soft serene tune playing from a lime-coloured radio beside her bed.

"Ah you will be fine. Hester over here was watching you. She was *very* scared." A doctor was saying beside her, Sally didn't realise that a doctor was there.

"Her name is Hester?" Sally glanced at the doctor, puzzled, why hadn't Hester ever told her?

The doctor nodded and left the room.

Hester was sitting further away on a stool, playing a game, she held a device in which she pushed her finger on rapidly.

"W-what are you doing? Screens are a disturbance, the doctors should've given you a toy to play with but, alas, we do work in a place of infuriating doctors." Sally groaned again; Hester squealed cheerfully, totally ignoring Sally's remarks.

Sally let herself collapse on the bed; how could Juana just die so quickly? Nothing was wrong with her, was it? Or was Juana hiding her illness to remain at work and sustain her dominating repute?

An hour later, Sally found herself at the sickbay room, in her PPE clothes, Hester was gone and not with her, Sally was confused...and... for the first time...anxious for her.

She was hurrying out the door, distressed, looking everywhere for Hester. She noticed a doctor talking to Hester, but Sally thought it was important so hid behind a wall and listened.

It wasn't just any Doctor.

It was Wayne. Uriah's best friend (even Uriah hated Sally).

Wayne probably knew that Sally was closely associated with Hester, even though Sally didn't get along with Hester, Sally was conceited and had a hatred for children.

Though, Sally has to interfere.

Chapter 3 – Sally Loves Revenge

Sally shoved aside all the hastening doctors, she stamped her foot in fury, Hester glanced at Sally with glee, she ran to her and hugged firmly.

"What are you doing here, Sally? You are snobbish and nosy, leave and go to the DDO's office. I swear that Juana had called you. Hm?" Wayne stepped his foot, gawking at Sally with a smug face.

"I should ask you, what did *you* tell the child? We're in a crisis and you're going around telling kids about how I am such an arrogant and rude person, but that's just in your eyes!" Sally decreed, Wayne sniffed evilly, and stood up straight.

"Nobody likes you Sally Harriet. We all think you're here just to pass time, get your money, and scamper back home. We all know that Harriet." He glanced at Sally, with a look of evil glistening in his eyes, Sally had an impulsive urge to storm off, but she'd look frail.

"Ha-ha!" Sally sardonically said. "You're not hilarious, Wayne. Now I'm asking again, what did you tell the child? You don't give me a respectful reply, you will regret your decision. Now tell me." Sally bobbed her foot, staring at Wayne with narrowed eyes.

Wayne looked tense. He was nervy as he thought of Sally's punishment, everyone knew that even though Sally was an introverted and sullen lady, she could also be the most intrepid and dangerous.

"I didn't say anything Harriet, I swear- "Wayne stuttered but dropped to the ground, as he felt a shove.

Sally had pushed him, her hands still dangling mid-air. She gazed at Wayne with a nasty smirk, and hassled off, Hester galloping behind too.

"Bravery. That's bravery!" Hester was yelling joyfully, all the doctors turned their heads to look at Hester, who was prancing, Sally blushed fearfully and ran off like it wasn't her business.

Sally sat at the cafeteria chair, charmed and pleased by making Wayne suffer just like Sally had to undergo bullying and mocking from him and Uriah.

"So, what did you do after? Tell someone, or fight even more?" Alicia had questioned her, interested in the brawl more than the steamy and sizzling pasta laying in front of her.

"No, just ran off. Didn't want Wayne running up to the chiefs about a fight. I'll probably fired." Sally replied, kidding around with her food using her fork.

"He'll be too stupid to do that. We know you're a feisty one, Sal." A lady next to Sally articulated and chortled, it was a girl with lengthy golden hair, hazel eyes and a kind smile. It was Arlo, the nurse.

"Arlo, good to see you. Why have you been off work for so long?" Alicia asked her, Arlo glanced at Alicia and chuckled worriedly.

"I was sick. Got the Deathbell disease. Had severe coughing. Or..." Arlo put her hand on her chin, and looked upwards, as if thinking.

"I promise the infection is certainly not communicable. The infection was from an animal, I think from a sort of insect." Alicia gazed at Sally in astonishment, Sally shrugged.

"You're a doctor and you don't even know whether a severe disease is non-communicable or transmittable. Funny." A girl joined the table, she was being swarmed by all her friends who were texting and sitting around her, she spoke in a snotty way, and grunted whenever Sally and her friends said something incorrect.

It was Lilith. An obnoxious lady who spoke to everyone in an egotistical and impolite way. She was hypocritical as she critiqued and protested about other people being "insolent" or "bad-mannered" even though she was all those things herself.

"If you know the answer, Lilith. Why don't you say it, know-it-all?" Alicia grumbled, Lilith looked at Sally and her, acting as if she was insulted.

"What did you call me?" Lilith stood up, her tone upraised, her voice even more disrespectful than usual.

"Alicia, sit down. Yeah, she called you a know-it-all, is that something to be miserable of?" Sally stood up as well, everyone looked at them interestedly, some stood up to observe from a distance, muttering and snickering, their voices stifled by their hands, making sure not to get into what they called the 'Bratty Business'.

The 'Bratty Business' was a gigantic commotion of trendy people versus other trendy people who were considered to 'steal-the-spotlight', Lilith and Sally were one of the leading protagonists in this drama.

"Well, if it isn't 'Single-minded Sally'. You think I'm frightened of some irresponsible girl who thinks she's superior to everyone else?" Lilith enquired, her eyebrows raised, and she laughed, glancing haughtily at Sally.

"I'm pleased you've finally said some things about me, yet I couldn't care less, but alas, you do not realise that it is just a replication of your own self." Sally chuckled, everyone joined in and sniggered too, it was shocking, Sally never had anyone on her side before, yes, her Mother was right, it felt good to be supported by others you really didn't socialise with.

Lilith thrusted the table heatedly and stormed from the room, her friends trailing behind her, everyone applauded for Sally, some cheered, even the dinner servers grinned and giggled.

The 'Bratty Business' fuss was finally over.

Who knew you required a few words to end something so immense?

Chapter 4 – New Manager Alice

Sally was relaxing at the refectory when she was called to approach the manager's office with Hester.

They sauntered to the office, Hester humming and Sally thinking.

Everyone knew Juana had died. It was a gloomy day yesterday, everyone herding around her grave, whispering praises and blessings for her afterlife. Sally was standing there; she and Hester had viewed Juana's death; it was frightening yet plausible.

How was her death so swift? How did she even die like that? A flicker of light, and she was dead on the floor; maybe it was thunder? Or electricity? The wires were a bit of a problem as of the living crisis and increasing hospital bills and transactions.

The hospital was going down.

So many were nauseous and needed treatment to get better. Person after person gushed into the sanatorium doors, complaining and groaning in pain from the illness.

It was a creepy sight to see as people stirred around like half-dead zombies, some resting on the floor in agony, their bodies twisting like fiends, like an immortal, so uncanny.

Sally was gazing at the oak door of the office. A gilded plate with the name Alice Larson, it used to be Juana's name.

Sally paced into what was once Juana's office, but now some surly-looking lady had superseded her in a blink of an eye.

"Hello there, Sally! I'm Alice, nice to meet you both." she said kindly, her face broke into a gigantic convivial smile.

The lady got up, hurried up to her and shook Sally's hand, she patted Hester on the head, complimenting her.

Then she stumbled back to her seat and transformed into a sombre face, a stiff posture, and a stern tone.

"We are aware of the two terrible and disturbing news that has broken through our medical staff. The death of former manager Juanita, and the still-happening Death-bell disease. Juana was an amazing lady, a friend of mine, but has sadly passed due to an electrical burst." Alice sternly said, glancing at the two wide-eyed young people standing in front of them.

"We were there, though. How did we not die?" Sally questioned, perplexed and slightly sceptical.

"It is a miracle! Let us not jinx reality and continue living our life!" Alice again smiled at them and laughed.

Why is she laughing about death? I guess that's just her character.

"Oh dear, I'm not laughing about death!" Alice stated as she stared at Sally.

She didn't reply.

Mind reader, odd. I thought those folks disappeared long ago.

"Nuh-uh Sally. We 'folk' have not disappeared, and we are still here, to take over-", Alice stopped mid-way through her sentence.

"You may leave now! Bye-bye!" Alice rushed to the door and slammed it as Sally and Hester left, both puzzled.

What if...Alice...is responsible for this post-apocalypse?

Sally dropped Hester to the playhouse.

"Now, you stay here, and behave! I don't want the nice lady who is supervising you children to complain, ok?" Sally said, Hester nodded, let out a loud 'yahoo' and hopped inside the ball pit.

"Thanks Beth." Sally waved, Beth the sitter smiled as she skipped around with one of the children.

Sally hurried to the staff room, where her friends all sat, gossiping at a table, eating ice-cream.

"Arlo! Alicia! And Rita?" Sally squealed, her best friend Rita was there, it was 2 weeks, and Rita was absent, she was on a vacation in Italy.

"And how was Italy?" Sally questioned Rita, also budging next to her.

Rita was one of the finest doctors; she was also a sportsperson before her grandfather fell ill and was diagnosed with a disease, which inspired her to join the medical profession.

"Spain was a blast! We went swimming at the beach and even did a few camping trips." Rita cheerfully sighed as she pondered about her running at the beach free, only her, her family and the vast land of sand and water.

"We've been coping with the Deathbell disease. Everyone's coming to us, as we're a high-end hospital." Sally replied, everyone groaned except Rita.

"I've heard about it. Is it that bad?" Rita asked, glancing around at everyone's faces.

Everyone nodded.

Chapter 5 – Suspicions

Sally told her crew of friends that they should meet during tomorrow's break.

"Listen, I have suspicions about the manager, Alice-" Sally stated, but Alicia interrupted.

"Off with the superstitions again, are you, Sally?" Alicia giggled, but Sally soughed.

"She's a mind reader! A literal demon-girl!" Sally yelled back; everyone from the other tables eyed Sally oddly.

"How can she be a mind reader, Sal? Are you insane?" Rita responded, peeking at Alicia, who jostled her shoulders.

Sally squelched her head in her arms, irritated at how she was labelled to constantly create lies.

That's a downside of being sullen, grouchy and silent.

"Oh...it's ok, Sally. I'll speak to her; you guys remain here." Arlo patted Sally's shoulder whilst Sally grumbled as her friend led her out of the room.

"I believe you; I know that Alice girl is strange. Now tell me, how do you have proof that first she's a mind reader? And if she's part of you know, anything odd?" Arlo questioned enthusiastically; Sally squealed happily.

"Come with me..." Sally clutched Arlo's hand, and they stepped gradually and cautiously to the lab room, where a gruff voice spoke inside; the door, luckily, was ajar.

"I told you, Rochelle, I need the mixtures ready for shipping! We can't afford to lose a million in profit; we need 6 batches of that, and if it isn't ready by 10 minutes, Silas won't be glad!" Alice was yelling, and a skittish voice of a youthful girl spoke in reply.

"Yes, Madam Amaris. I will right away." The girl replied gloomily, and then a rackety clatter of glass shifted around tables.

"Yes! Yes! We'll get millions and become wealthy. Just for spreading some stupid disease! We'll be rich, and Rochelle, we shall move on a yacht, or only *I* shall move on the yacht; you can be with Silas." Alice chortled wickedly whilst Rochelle whined.

Footsteps entered the lab from a door.

"Is my haul ready for dispatch?" A man asked; his voice was solemn but somewhat soft.

"Yes Silas. It is ready to be taken to the ship. Rochelle, please carry the crates to the ship, and get a move on!" Alice yelled at the girl, who grabbed the crate and followed Silas.

Alice exited the room; her malicious grin stretched ear to ear.

Arlo and Sally entered the room; their jaws dropped open.

Crates and crates were supplied with glass containers of blue liquid. The lab room was in a poor state, smashed glass embedded in the plaster, paint splatters across the room tiles and countertops, and chalk and spray paint blanketing the wall.

Sally and Arlo reached for a crate and saw a sign.

FRAGILE: DEATHBELL VIRUS FOR DISPATCH

"What the hell?!" Arlo was about to scream, but Arlo hushed her.

"Stop causing chaos, Arlo." Sally whispered, "No one has to know about this, we'll be in trouble, and perhaps blamed of creating this. We are supposed to be heroes, not villains, understand?"

Arlo nodded, still dazed from what she had witnessed.

They crept out from the room, both surprised, Arlo's face was pallid, and her jaw hanged upon, while Sally had an aloof face, her disbelief incarcerated inside her.

Chapter 6 – A Plan and A Sad Goodbye

Sally and Arlo departed the room to fetch Hester.

"She's been well-behaved, even had a lollipop, she was that good!" Beth said, as Sally smiled at Hester and took her from the room.

"What should we do? Alice is a Madam!? Oh, and her name isn't even Alice, its Amaris." Arlo articulated, and Sally shook her head.

"Keep it down, Arlo; you need to stop-" Sally halted mid-way, as two ladies arrived in front of her; one was one of the receptionists, Larisa, and the other was unknown.

"I'm so sorry Sally, but Hester must be taken away from you, due to your caring months has been completed." Larisa murmured; she said it slow and gradually.

Sally's heart broke.

"Why? When?" Sally stuttered; Hester glanced at Sally sadly.

"We've found her a mother who is interested in her for adoption. It's the lady over here, her name's Melissa." Larisa replied to Sally; they both understood it would be challenging to let her go.

"Hey! I'm Melissa Bardot, and I would like to adopt this child from your care." Melissa said sweetly, she glanced at Hester, and Hester beamed.

"She's not mine; I-I found her; you can take her, its fine." Sally answered. She shifted Hester towards Melissa, and the lady grinned.

"Thank you, Sally." Melissa and Larisa said, Larisa told Melissa to go.

"I know it's difficult; Hester is a lovely girl. But she'll always remember you. So, take it as a win-win." Clarissa placed a soothing hand on Sally's shoulder and grinned.

And that was Hester's story.

"What are we going to do!? The ship is leaving in 6 minutes according to our calculations!" Arlo shrieked; she began to scamper around, all panicky and agitated.

"Don't worry; I need only one tool. A superweapon." Sally said, a grin displaying on her face.

"And what would that be?" Arlo requested, stammering, wishing it wouldn't be "that".

"The Fusion Flux. Bring it here, Arlo." Sally stood up, her fists at the ready, her eyes shone with power.

"They can try to kill me. But they will not kill the citizens...and Hester."

Chapter 7 – Running To The Ship

Arlo brought in the large gun, a stunning metal rifle; gems and crusted diamonds shone, and lava could be heard splashing in its interiors.

"A beauty, isn't it Arlo?" Sally said, smoothing the rifle with her pale fingers.

Arlo grinned nervously; she shook her head in doubt that this was all a fantasy, sympathizing with herself and brushing her arms.

Sally and Arlo ran outside. There were seconds before the ship would vacate, and Amaris was roaring until she noticed them. They charged towards Amaris and Silas, though Silas witnessed them with a peek from his spectacles and quickened to them, his hand in the air, and gushing from it was an electric blue star.

"Sally! Get away from them!" Alicia could be heard yelling at her, and Arlo forced Sally away.

Sally stood up and shot from her gun; a gigantic lava orb charged at Silas's face, boiling it; a scream, a blow, and Silas were on the floor, wiggling in discomfort.

Amaris stepped forward.

"You may have beaten Silas. But you shall never defeat me, though I am eternal. Your life will end today, while I will take it as amusement!" Amaris screamed at them, and then a filmy glow engulfed her, and she exploded.

Dead? Oh no, she's not dead. It just gets worse.

A giant devilish ogre stepped out from the darkness; it had verdant sludgy skin like a snail, its hair was a shaggy blonde like a horse's mane, its teeth were of a vampire's, and its eyes were huge and cerulean, bloodthirsty and voracious. It was Amaris. It growled and boomed, chucked aside the ship, seized the crates and flung it to the city; Sally heard riots from the city, howls and the sound of an early demise. Sally kept on shooting and shooting fireballs at the immense beast, each roar deafened Sally, but she pushed on, forcing herself forward. Amaris eventually got more vulnerable; it dropped to the ground, twitching and shouting, big globes of water seeping from its viper eyes, its teeth bare.

"That's what you get, when you mess with Sally!" Sally yelled, chuckling evilly at the brute, who whimpered in response.

A last fireball shot at the eyes of the beast, it let out a thunderous rumble and a beastly sneer, then its talons stretched upwards to the sky, and it died, the dust from the fight layering it. Sally's face was concealed in dirt and scratches, her PPE uniform all tattered up from the fight, she was fatigued, and ravenous, but a huge toothy grin was stretched from ear to ear on her face. Alicia, Arlo and a mob of doctors cheered and rushed to her, but there was one final step.

"I will bring the CEO and the police. You are all to make an antidote for the Deathbell disease." Sally articulated, Alicia and Arlo exchanged a look.

"But we don't know what to use, we've been trying to make a remedy, but they all are just disappointments. We used so many elements and ways, but it just flops!" A doctor from the crowd yelled, but Sally shook her head.

"Here, Alicia, take these notes. I've had it barred up in my draw, it is some of the elements that we as doctors have used in some of our treatments that have been efficacious. Like when the flu came, and stuff. Keep it safe, it'll guide you all when making medicines" Sally articulated, she handed Alicia a scrunched-up sheet of paper, they both smiled and Alicia, Arlo and the other doctors rushed through the doors to the lab room.

"And that's that sorted...let me call the police." But before Sally dialled the number, a pompous, irritated man strolled from the doors to Sally.

He was robed in a grey linen suit with black streaks, he wore a stylish red tie popped in his collar, he had a monocle on, and wore a grey hat.

"Mr. Eldrick Whitty, the Chief Executive Officer of this hospital. The police will not be needed now, but maybe later. What is this mess? And what is that?" Mr Whitty shrieked and indicated at the resting beast, its one eye half open, blood trickling from its cracked and parched lips.

"That is Alice the beast or should I say, Amaris. Amaris has wreaked chaos, sir. We have discovered that she and Silas has been transmitting illegal bottles of the Deathbell disease, and giving to our calculations and note-taking, *they* have been the cause for the endemic that has arose, Mr Whitty." Sally clarified to him, Mr Whitty looked traumatised and pale, he smacked his palm on his forehead, scratched his chin, and gazed at Sally with intent of listening to her.

"This is an outrage, these poor civilians have been suffering due to these two freaks, and us, we have been economically damaged, our fellow colleagues have been mentally ill from exhaustion. These two if alive, should have been put to jail straight away. Is the fellow gentleman over there involved?" Mr Whitty questioned Sally, he was pointing at Silas who was also dead on the floor, his jaw hanged open.

"Yes, he is Silas, he is dead but was involved, he actually was the protagonist and antagonist in this whole situation, he was the chief, the one who would've proposed money to Amaris. Amaris also had a slave, a young girl called Rochelle. I believe Rochelle was quite distressed and was threatened to be sent to Silas after Amaris obtained the profit." Sally said, she felt like the apprentice of Mr Whitty, though he just nodded and bobbed his head.

"Illegal vendorship is one of the worst cases of crime in our history of this city. We should apprise the citizens that who and what was the cause of the disease, we mustn't distress and anger them, for that would be worse for us and the government. Do not worry, Sally, for you have been the redeemer of us all, you shall be rewarded for this support and deed, and though you may be morose, you are our hero." Mr Whitty shook hands with Sally, who acknowledged her and Sally grinned, the man left without another word, and Sally strolled as well behind with pleasure. She was the hero.

Chapter 8 – Antidotes

Sally supported the team in constructing an antidote. They all worked hard and were drained, but they never gave up, and that was all because of Sally.

Sally wasn't her usual self these days, she was encouraging, content and glad. Sally praised the doctors even if they flopped and if *they* sulked, she would be there to sympathise them.

"Come on guys, you can all do it! We are doctors, and we will rejoice once this problem is solved!" Sally would say, and like an activist, she would march around with her friends, walking into rooms and fluttering flags that had prints of quotes of inspiration.

A week flew by and the day came of joy, it was when Sally was strolling around, when she heard a loud scream of joy in a nearby lab, all the doctors including Sally rushed into the room, curious of the commotion.

"I've done it! I have the medicine; I have the cure!" The doctor Maria, yelled, and danced with delight, she held a bottle of pink liquid, and she poured it on the Deathbell blood sample and instantly the thick blood became a pure liquid, Maria joyfully danced, and everyone celebrated, assembling around and running through the corridors, shouting into rooms that the problem was done, the crisis is solved!

Sally was grinning with pride, knowing that she had played an integral role in this success. She hugged her colleagues and chuckled with them, feeling a sense of amity as she ran around happily.

As they all sat down to relax after the long days of hard work, Sally took a moment to reflect on the past week. She realized that even though they had faced setbacks, they never gave up because of perseverance and a little luck.

Observing the pink liquid that had just been revealed, Sally sighed with relief. This antidote would save a myriad of lives and place a close to the crisis that had been looming over them for weeks.

Sally and her friends hanged out as she decided to take a break, in the meanwhile, many people were travelling to get the medicine, and in a few weeks, people were getting better.

Sally returned home after a long and exhausting week at the hospital, feeling drained yet fulfilled. As soon as she stepped inside, her phone started buzzing, and her inbox was flooded with messages and emails.

She groaned in annoyance but decided to check who the hell kept on spamming her inbox.

"Ughhhh...I literally organised my emails into sections just a few days ago...who in the world is sending me these messages!" She articulated, as she sat crossly on her bed.

As she sat down to check her messages, Sally was stunned by the outpouring of support and gratitude from people who had heard about her work. There were messages from former patients and their families, thanking her for her hard work and commitment, and from co-workers and friends, commending her for her motivation to other workers.

Truthfully, her colleagues were agitated and exhausted from the amount of patients pouring into the hospital, complaining that they were gravely ill, the antidote was still in a process for reproduction, so Sally had decided to send these duplicates to pharmacists to dispatch immediately to people who were ill, this eased the burden on doctors, who were now able to work at a sufficient time length and support a suitable amount of patients.

As the night wore on, Sally continued to receive messages and calls from people expressing their appreciation. Though she was fatigued, Sally couldn't help but grin as every email rush into her inbox, sufficing her with joy.

Days went past, Sally was greeted and meted by people on the streets, hugging her and thanking her for support.

"Because of you, my daughters and sons survived from that horrendous disease. You are such an angel! Such an angel!" Some mothers and fathers sobbed, they clasped on to their children, laughing and sighing cheerfully.

Chapter 9 – Hester's Illness

Hester's mother was anxious when her daughter came home from school complaining of feeling unwell. She had heard of a disease going around and that it was cured, but she still feared. Hester's symptoms were typical of the disease - a high fever, severe headache, and a red rash. She rushed her to the hospital, where she was immediately placed in a private room. The doctors had already seen dozens of patients with the same symptoms, and they knew exactly what it was, it wasn't Deathbell, it was an extremely rare virus called Venerosis.

Venerosis was a rare but deadly disease caused by a toxin found in the Veneroi plant. The plant grew wild in the nearby woods, and it was not rare for people to accidentally ingest it. The disease was highly infectious, and the hospital had set up a special ward to deal with this. Hester was one of the first patients to be admitted to the ward.

Despite the doctors' knowledge of the disease, Hester's condition continued to deteriorate rapidly. Her fever spiked to perilous levels, and she was emotional with pain. The rash on her skin became unhealthier, and she was unable to keep any food down. The doctors did everything they could to keep her contented, but there was no cure yet. All they could do was to try and manage her symptoms.

Hester's mother was forlorn. She spent every moment by her side, praying for a miracle. She watched as her daughter grew feebler by the day, hardly able to move or speak. The hospital staff did their best to console Hester's mother, but they could see the despair in her mother's eyes.

Weeks went by, and Hester's condition did not improve. She became increasingly frail, barely clinging to life. The staff were extremely worried, and all they did was console her that she would be fine, but they knew that her time was running out. They called in a specialist, hoping that he might be able to offer some hope.

The specialist was a tall man, his name was Mr Walker, he examined Hester carefully, taking more samples of her blood. He confirmed what the other doctors had suspected - Hester had contracted Venerosis. He explained to her mother that the disease was extremely rare, and that there was no known cure. He could only offer pain relief and comfort care.

Days turned into weeks, and Hester's condition continued to worsen. Her breathing became shallow and strenuous, and her skin became icy and clammy. She was barely conscious, drifting in and out of delirium. Her mother knew that the end was near, but she could not accept it. She cried for a miracle, but nothing ever came.

Finally, Hester slipped away, her body succumbing to the ravages of the disease. Her mother was inconsolable, grief-stricken by the loss of her adored daughter. The hospital staff sympathised the desperate mother, but they knew that nothing could ease the pain of losing a child. Hester's life had been cut short by an irregular and lethal disease, leaving behind a family and a society devastated by grief.

Sally was informed Hester had died.

Sally hurried to the room in her PPE, tears gushing out from her eyes, she gazed at the mother who was weeping, Sally gazed at Hester, who was laying lifeless in the bed, her expression miserable and petrified, her skin so pale from that beast that had possessed her body.

Sally sobbed and wept, trying not to remember the days that they both had, the painful memories that stabbed Sally's heart anytime she thought of it.

It was one of the times where her emotions were irrepressible.

Chapter 10 – How It All Started

Sally was a doctor who had dedicated her life to the medical profession. She had always been cranky, but still decided to pursue a career in medicine. She worked tirelessly day and night, treating patients and saving lives. Her hard work and dedication had earned her a reputation as one of the best doctors in town.

Recently, there had been an outbreak of a deadly disease in the area. The disease had spread rapidly, and many people had fallen ill. Sally was among the doctors who were working round the clock to find a cure for the disease. She spent hours researching and consulting with other doctors to find a way to contain the disease and save as many lives as possible.

Finally, after weeks of hard work and willpower, A lady called Maria found a cure for the disease. It was a moment of triumph for Sally and everyone involved in the fight against the disease.

Maria stood proud, and Sally gave her gratitude.

As the news spread, people began to celebrate. There were parties and parades, and everyone was appreciative that the disease had been contained. Sally was invited to speak at a public event, where she was praised for her role in being one of the most considerate doctors.

Standing in front of a crowd of people, Sally laughed and grinned with edginess, as the swarming paparazzi took pictures of her.

She spoke about the long hours of work, the restless nights, and the sacrifices that she and her colleagues had made to unearth a cure. She thanked everyone who had supported them along the way and accredited the bravery of those who had fallen ill. Sally's speech was met with a thunderous round of applause, and she felt dazed by the support and gratitude of the community.

It was a moment she would never forget.

After the event, Sally went back to work, treating patients as usual. But this time, there was a sense of relief and joy in the air. Patients who had been infected with the disease were now recovering, and the hospital was jam-packed with beams and laughter.

As Sally walked through the hospital corridors, she beamed at everyone as they smiled at her, she was not her sullen self anymore. She had devoted her life to the medical profession, and now she had played a significant role in saving many lives.

The memory of the outbreak, cure and the death of Hester would always stay with Sally, reminding her of the power of determination, hard work, and the human spirit.

Chapter 11 – Greeting A Grave

Sally had always been enthused by the strength of her young patient, Hester. Hester had been diagnosed with a rare and aggressive form of Venerosis at a very young age. Despite the grim prognosis, Hester had fought hard, never giving up hope or losing her spirit.

Sally had spent uncountable hours with Hester, trying distinctive treatments and therapies in an effort to help her beat the disease. Even though the odds were stacked against them, Sally never gave up on her patient. Hester's courage and determination had touched Sally deeply, and she had grown to care for the young girl as if she were her own. Sadly, despite their best efforts, Hester had lost her battle. Her death had hit

Sally hard, and she found it difficult to come to terms with the loss of her young patient.

Months after Hester's passing, Sally decided to visit her grave. She had never been one for sentimental gestures, but something inside her pushed her to go and pay her respects to the brave little girl who had touched her life so intensely.

As Sally stood before Hester's grave, she snivelled. Sadness for the loss of such a young life, but also respect for the astonishing strength and courage that Hester had shown throughout her illness.

Sally spoke to Hester, thanking her for inspiring her and for teaching her about the true meaning of love and resilience. She praised Hester for the impact she had made on her life and for the lessons she had taught her.

As Sally walked away from the grave, she hummed as she had found her sense of tranquillity. She knew that Hester's memory would always live on, inspiring her to continue fighting for her patients and to never give up hope, even in the face of the toughest challenges.

As Sally returned home from visiting Hester's grave, her heart was heavy with grief. She had lost many patients throughout her career, but Hester had been different. The young girl's spirit had touched Sally deeply, and she had grown to care for her like her own child.

As she sat down in her living room, Sally tried to brush off the sadness that had enveloped her. She was stunned by the weight of the loss, and she knew that she needed to find a way to cope with her grief.

She looked around her living room, taking in the familiar surroundings that had always brought her comfort. But today, even her cosy home felt empty and hollow. Sally thought back to the lessons that Hester had taught her about resilience and hope. She realized that she needed to find a way to honour Hester's memory and to carry on the young girl's legacy of strength and courage.

Sally decided to take action. She picked up her phone and started to research charities and organizations that worked towards finding a cure for the rare form of illness that Hester had battled.

After much research, Sally found an organization that aligned with her values and that supported research into the disease that had claimed Hester's life. She decided to make a donation in Hester's memory, hoping that it would make a difference in the lives of other children who were fighting the same battle.

As Sally made the donation, she felt a sense of peace. She knew that Hester's memory would live on through the work of the organization, and that her young patient's legacy of strength and hope would continue to inspire others.

Sally sat down once again, feeling lighter and more at ease. She knew that her grief would never fully go away, but she also knew that she could honour Hester's memory in a meaningful way. She made a vow to always remember Hester and to strive to be the best doctor she could be, inspired by the young girl's unwavering spirit and resilience.

Chapter 12 – Last Resort

Sally grew much older, but she still sustained to be an active member of her community, sharing her knowledge and experience with younger generations. She had had children of her own, and she was determined to instil in them the values of compassion, dedication, and resilience that had guided her throughout her career.

She desired for her daughters and sons to be inspired by her, and to plant a seed of gentleness in their hearts, it was effective and as her children grew older and older, they themselves became doctors, dentists, botanists and so on.

One day, as Sally sat down with her children, she began to tell them the story of a pandemic that had swept the world many years ago. She spoke of the fear and uncertainty that had gripped the population, and of the countless lives that had been lost to the disease.

But she also spoke of the courage and determination of healthcare workers and volunteers who had worked tirelessly to fight the pandemic and to care for those who were sick. Sally shared with her children her own experiences during that time, of the long hours she had worked, the challenging decisions she had made, and the sacrifices she had witnessed. Sally's children listened with rapt attention as she spoke, amazed by the stories of heroism and sacrifice that their mother had witnessed. They were proud of their mother and inspired by her dedication to helping others, even in the most difficult of circumstances.

As Sally finished her story, she looked at her children with a sense of pride and hope. She knew that the lessons she had shared with them would stay with them for a lifetime, and that they would carry on the legacy of compassion and resilience that she had worked so hard to build. Sally's children, in turn, would pass on these lessons to their own children, and the cycle of compassion and dedication would continue. Sally felt a sense of peace knowing that her life's work would have a lasting impact on future generations.

As she looked out the window at the world around her, Sally knew that there were still many challenges ahead, but she was confident that with the right mindset and the right values, anything was possible. She smiled at her children, feeling grateful for the love and joy that they had brought into her life, and for the opportunity to pass on the lessons of her own experiences to a new generation.

Sally had always believed in the power of education and communication, and she had made it her mission to help spread accurate information about health and wellness to as many people as possible. As she grew even more older, she became even more committed to this goal, knowing that the more people understood about health and disease, the better equipped they would be to stay healthy and to take care of those around them.

She began giving talks and lectures to community groups and schools, sharing her own experiences and insights and helping to dispel myths and misinformation about health and medicine. She also worked with local health clinics and hospitals, volunteering her time to help patients and to train new doctors and nurses.

Sally's perseverance to health education earned her many accolades and honours, but she never lost sight of the importance of her work. She knew that there was still so much to be done, and she remained devoted to her mission even as she grew older and her health began to decline.

Despite her advancing age, Sally continued to work tirelessly, always striving to make a difference in the world. She knew that every moment was precious, and she never wasted a single one. Even as her own health began to falter, she remained focused on the needs of others, always putting the needs of her patients and her community first.

One day, as Sally sat in her garden, enjoying the warm sunshine on her face, she reflected on her life's work. She thought of all the people she had helped over the years, and of the many challenges she had faced and overcome.

She felt a sense of peace knowing that she had done everything in her power to make the world a better place. And yet, she knew that there was still so much more to be done.

Sally's thoughts were interrupted by the sound of her granddaughter's voice calling out to her from the house. Sally grinned and stood up, feeling grateful for the love and joy that her family brought into her life.

As she made her way back to the house, Sally knew that her work was not yet done. There were still so many people in the world who needed help, who needed someone to care for them and to fight for their well-being.

But she also knew that she had passed on her knowledge and her values to the next generation, and that they would carry on her work long after she was gone. She felt a sense of peace and satisfaction knowing that her legacy would live on, and that her life's work would continue to make a difference in the world for generations to come.

As Sally entered the house, her granddaughter ran up to her, giving her a warm hug. Sally smiled, feeling grateful for the love and joy that her family brought into her life.

Together, they sat down to share a meal, talking and laughing and enjoying each other's company. And as they talked, Sally felt a deep sense of contentment knowing that her life had been filled with purpose and meaning, and that she had made a real difference in the world.

As the evening drew to a close, Sally's granddaughter hugged her tightly, thanking her for all that she had done and for the lessons that she had taught her. Sally smiled, feeling grateful for the opportunity to share her knowledge and experience with the next generation.

As she made her way to bed that night, Sally felt a sense of peace and contentment. She knew that her time in this world was limited, but she also knew that she had done everything in her power to make a difference. And that was all that she could ever ask for.

As she shut her eyes, Sally thought of all the people she had helped over the years, and of the many challenges she had faced and overcome. She knew that her legacy would live on, and that the lessons she had taught would continue to inspire and guide others.

Sally woke up early the next morning, feeling grateful for another day. She made her way to the kitchen, where her daughter was already up, making coffee.

"Good morning, Mom," her daughter said, giving her a hug.

"Good morning, dear," Sally replied, returning the hug. "How did you sleep?"

"Great, thanks," her daughter said. "I was thinking about what you were saying last night, about the pandemic you helped to fight. I was wondering if you could tell me more about it?"

Sally smiled, feeling gratifying for the opportunity to share her experiences with her daughter. They sat down at the kitchen table, and Sally began to tell her daughter about the pandemic, describing the challenges she faced and the lessons she learned.

As they talked, Sally smiled at her and patted her shoulder with a deep sense of pride knowing that her daughter was interested in her work and her experiences. She knew that she had passed on her values and her passion for helping others to the next generation, and that they would continue to make a difference in the world long after she was gone.

After breakfast, Sally and her daughter decided to take a walk in the park. As they ambled along the paths, they chattered and laughed, enjoying each other's company and the beauty of the natural world around them. Sally smiled, knowing that she had passed on her values and her love for the world to her daughter. She felt grateful for the many blessings in her life, including her family, her health, and her life's work.

As they made their way back to the house, Sally felt a sense of sadness knowing that her time in this world was limited. But she also felt a sense of hope, knowing that her legacy would live on, and that the lessons she had taught would continue to inspire and guide others for generations to come.

She arrived at the house, Sally's family replied to her warmly, grateful for her presence in their lives. Together, they sat down to share a meal, talking and laughing and enjoying each other's company.

As the evening drew to a close, Sally felt a deep sense of peace and contentment. She knew that her life had been filled with purpose and meaning, and that she had made a real difference in the world.

As she closed her eyes that night, Sally thought of all the people she had helped over the years, and of the many challenges she had faced and overcome. She felt a sense of pride knowing that her legacy would live on, and that her life's work would continue to make a difference in the world for generations to come.

And as she drifted off to sleep, Sally felt indebted for the love and joy that her family brought into her life, knowing she was blessed to be living a life filled with purpose and experience.

She was ready for the next day.

But she didn't wake up the next morning.

Part 2 – The Aftermath

Chapter 1: The Beginning Of Another Adventure

Sally's children had now reached adulthood. Their minds still carried the permanent imprint of their mother's narratives and accounts of a pandemic that had occurred half a century ago. With their mother's passing, they were entrusted with the task of reshaping their emerging world.

The eldest daughter, Eleanor Harriet aged 28, resided in Surrey and had started a family of her own. Sally's son, Aaron, pursued his medical training in Manchester, finding boundless inspiration in the multitude of photographs capturing his mother's life. The second-to-last daughter, Lori, lived in Hertfordshire, where her dual passions for art and nursing intertwined.

The youngest of the siblings was Arinel, a 24-year-old residing in a modest home with her own family. She had two children, a mischievous yet eager boy named Caspian and an intrepid girl called Lycian. Caspian and Lycian brimmed with enthusiasm, sometimes exhibiting naughtiness, while at other times, eagerly listening to their grandmother's pandemic tales.

Lycian was the keenest child, Caspian was more mischievous and a little careless, even though he would listen, Lycian said "the stories go through one ear and out the other." Caspian took revenge on his sister later that night and tossed a pail of water on her whilst she was snoozing.

Lycian could be always heard reading in her room, nestled in her bed, gawking at her book with great admiration, her brother was a contrary, and he spent hours upon hours playing videogames even when his mother told him off, he would still use it secretly with less volume.

The truth was that some were more of a bookworm than an annoying want-to-be streamer for games, Lycian was a little horrible at times but was enormously daring, and Caspian also had a quality of bravery as he would always be the one watching crime mysteries on TV.

One day, Lycian was nestled in her book in the living room, reading a classic series of voyage books, whilst she strained to detach the muffled sound of her brother's puzzling game sounds. Unexpectedly, a deep rustle from the outside garden just arose, as if an animal was prowling around, ready for its next victim.

Lycian chucked the books aside, and took a step to the window, each step sufficed her with more and more fright, but also more curiosity trailed along.

She took a deep breath and opened the window, the cold breeze thrashed her auburn hair and she trembled, her hands became numb as she observed the garden like an owl, another rustle came but even louder, she squealed a little excitedly as she had felt as if the rustle itself was just calling her and awaiting her for her arrival.

She glanced back and stepped outside and closed the window, the evening sky was a glorious view but gawking at its remarkable beauty would've been a timewaster and time consumer, she ran to the bush and tore it away, her eyes filled with interest.

There, nestled amidst the foliage, was a small, worn leather journal. Lycian's heart skipped a beat as she gingerly picked it up, feeling the weight of history in her hands. The journal was weathered and aged, its pages yellowed with time, and its cover adorned with intricate engravings.

Lycian retreated back to her room, cradling the precious find like a cherished treasure. As she opened the journal, the musty scent of old paper filled the air, transporting her to a bygone era. The pages were filled with handwritten entries, penned in elegant cursive.

Lycian's eyes widened as she realized that this journal belonged to her grandmother, Sally. The entries chronicled her experiences during the pandemic, the very stories Lycian had grown up hearing. It was as if Sally's voice had been preserved within these fragile pages, waiting for Lycian to discover them.

Overwhelmed with excitement, Lycian began to read. The journal unveiled a world of uncertainty, resilience, and hope. Sally's words painted vivid pictures of communities coming together, acts of kindness that defied despair, and the unwavering strength of the human spirit. Lycian was captivated, her imagination running wild as she delved deeper into the stories.

Days turned into weeks, and Lycian became engrossed in her grandmother's narratives. She found herself transported to a time she had never known yet felt intimately connected to. Each entry brought the past to life, and Lycian was determined to preserve this legacy for future generations.

She began to transcribe the journal onto her laptop, carefully typing out every word, ensuring that the stories would endure in a digital form. As she worked diligently, Lycian couldn't help but ponder the significance of this newfound connection to her past.

Lycian hid her book from Caspian who was extremely nosy and kept spying through the keyhole to see Lycian's clandestine business.

"Go away, Caspian! Leave me alone, you weirdo!" She shouted at him and slammed the door with frustration.

Chapter 2 – Hidden Adventures:

Lycian's heart raced as she sat on the edge of her bed, her hands clutching the journal tightly. The weight of the secret she held felt both exhilarating and overwhelming. She knew she had to confide in someone, someone who would understand her yearning for adventure and the desire to explore the hidden depths of their family history. Lycian glanced at the closed door of her room; her mind made up.

Taking a deep breath, she walked to the living room where her mother, Arinel, sat engrossed in a book. Lycian approached her hesitantly, her voice filled with a mix of excitement and apprehension. "Mom, I have something important to share with you,"

Lycian began, her eyes shining with anticipation.

Arinel looked up from her book, curiosity spiralling in her eyes. "What is it, dear?" she asked, setting her book aside.

Lycian took a moment to gather her thoughts, then spoke earnestly, "I found Grandma Sally's journal, the one that contains all her stories about

the pandemic. It's an incredible treasure, Mom, and I want to embark on an adventure to discover the places and experiences she wrote about."
Arinel's eyebrows furrowed with concern. "An adventure? What kind of adventure, Lycian?" she asked, her voice filled with a mix of curiosity and worry.

Lycian's gaze met her mother's, and she saw a flicker of understanding in Arinel's eyes. "I want to travel to the places Grandma mentioned, experience the world as she did, and document my journey." Lycian explained, her voice tinged with both determination and vulnerability.

Arinel paused, processing Lycian's words. She understood her daughter's thirst for exploration, as well as the weight of the family history they now carried. After a moment, she sighed softly, a mix of concern and love in her voice. "Lycian, I can see how important this is to you. But you're still young and embarking on such an adventure alone could be risky. I worry for your safety."

Lycian nodded, understanding her mother's concerns. "I promise, Mother, I won't take any unnecessary risks. I'll be cautious, responsible, and I'll call you every day to let you know I'm safe. You have my word," she assured her mother.

Arinel's gaze softened as she looked at her determined daughter. She knew deep down that Lycian's spirit was untamed, and her longing for exploration was as much a part of her as the air she breathed. Arinel sighed and shook her head.

"No, I will not consent to that, Lycian. You are only 12 years old, and that is a young age, I shall not permit it." She shook her head again, and groaned at Lycian's exasperated but troubled reaction, Lycian thought she was old enough to venture herself, school was not an adventure, no, no, Lycian just considered it as a place to fairly waste your energy.

"But mother! I want to just like Grandmother! How is that fair? I'm sure Grandma Sally was allowed to at my age." Lycian justified, but Arinel became stressed and gazed at her with widened eyes.

"Lycian! I said, no! Just because your grandmother may have been allowed to do it, *her* parents knew *her* better, and it does not mean that I will allow you to do the same!" Arinel screeched and departed the room, leaving a utterly exasperated Lycian in the room, as Arinel unlocked the door, Lycian could notice Caspian glaring at her and sniggering uncontrollably, Lycian shoved him away and snickered as he dropped to the floor with a tumble and sat on her chair again, desperate and gloomy. "If she doesn't allow me, I'm going to have to allow myself." She grinned at herself evilly, and an hour later went to bed, a malevolent grin stretched ear to ear.

Chapter 3 – The Midnight Train For Departure

The moon hung high in the night sky, casting an ethereal glow over Lycian's room as she sat on her bed, the journal resting on her lap. The weight of her decision pressed upon her, but her longing for adventure burned brighter than ever. Arinel had said no, deeming the journey too risky, but Lycian couldn't ignore the call of her grandmother's stories.

Minutes ticked by, and Lycian's determination grew stronger. She knew that if she wanted to embark on this adventure, she would have to do it alone, in the dead of night when the world was asleep. Warily, she crammed a small bag with the essentials—clothes, a map, lunch, a flashlight, and, most importantly, Grandma Sally's journal.

She cringed at every tiptoe in her room, but still alert not to make a sound. Every creak of the floorboards felt like a deafening noise, threatening to expose her clandestine plan. But Lycian was resolved. She believed that this adventure would not only connect her to her family's past but also help her discover herself.

With her bag packed and the journal safely tucked away, Lycian took one last glance at her room. The familiar walls held memories of her childhood, but now they felt confining, suffocating her desire for exploration. She took a deep breath, reminding herself of the promise she made to her mother—to call every day, no matter what.

Soundlessly, Lycian unlocked her window, its hinges protesting with a faint squeak. She grimaced at the sound, freezing for a moment, but the house remained still, undisturbed. The night air was cool against her skin, carrying a sense of liberation. She slipped through the window, leaving behind the safety and familiarity of her childhood home.

Her heart pounded in her chest, Lycian was the only one standing like a freak in the garden, just her and the endless sky. She gazed up at the stars, their brilliance guiding her, and whispered a silent goodbye to the life she was leaving behind, at least temporarily. Her determination propelled her forward, urging her to embrace the unknown.

With each step, the world around her transformed. The once-familiar streets became a labyrinth of possibilities, a gateway to the stories that lay hidden within Grandma Sally's journal. Lycian walked in the shadows, guided by the faint glow of streetlights, and the quiet hum of the city as it slumbered.

Hours passed, and Lycian found herself on a train platform, the only soul waiting for the next departure. The weight of her decision pressed upon her, doubts threatening to erode her resolve. But as she clutched the journal close to her chest, she drew strength from the stories within its pages. They reminded her of the resilience and courage that ran in her blood.

As the train arrived, Lycian took a deep breath and stepped aboard, still in disbelief in what she had just done. The journey ahead was undefined, and the road would not always be smooth, but Lycian knew that this adventure was hers to embrace. She would unravel the hidden chapters of her family's history, discover her own strengths, and return home with a newfound understanding of who she was.

As the train was lugged away from the platform, Lycian rested against the window, watching her hometown fade into the distance. The night stretched out before her, brimming with possibilities and the promise of discovery. With each passing mile, she left behind the world she knew and ventured into the unknown, ready to create her own story, one that would intertwine with the legacy of her family and the tales hidden within Grandma Sally's cherished journal.

"A journal, eh? Is that Sally Harriet's?" A voice called, the voice was strong and Lycian span around to see a girl standing with flaxen hair, gawking at her with a combination of bewilderment, respect and content.

Chapter 4 – The Girl From Nowhere

Lycian settled into her seat on the train after standing for an hour, her mind filled stress of her unknown journey. She opened Grandma Sally's journal, immersing herself in the captivating stories of the past. Lost in her thoughts, she didn't notice the girl, who had asked her about the journal, had taken the seat beside her.

As the train rattled along, the girl glanced at the worn journal in Lycian's hands. Her eyes widened, a flicker of recognition crossing her face. "Is that the journal of Sally?"

Surprised, Lycian gazed up from the pages, her stare meeting the girl's. She faltered for a moment, shy on how to react to this unforeseen inquiry. "Um, yes. It belonged to my grandmother, Sally Harriet," Lycian responded, watchfully.

A smile tugged at the corners of the girl's lips. "I knew it! My grandmother, Alicia Fernford, was Sally's best friend. They used to share everything, including their stories from the pandemic. Alicia has mentioned that journal countless times," she exclaimed, her voice brimming with enthusiasm, all the passengers looked at Lycian and the girl, Lycian flushed in embarrassment

Lycian's curiosity sparked, and she leaned in closer. "Oh, whisper! Wait, you're Alicia Fern ford's granddaughter? That means our grandmothers were friends. Do you know any stories that they didn't write down in the journal?" she queried, excitement surging through her.

The girl bowed, her blonde hair cascading around her shoulders. "Yes, Alicia has shared a few stories with me over the years. She used to talk about Sally's courage during those challenging times and the adventures they embarked on together. It's incredible to think that their stories are intertwined," she responded, a hint of admiration in her voice, she had a little smug expression.

Despite the unexpected connection, Lycian found the girl's demeanour somewhat vexing, she thought she was a bit of an egotist.

There was an air of self-assuredness about her, as if she held a secret of her own. Lycian knew that the something was up, even with her innocent freckled face and wide indigo eyes. It was as if she had to prove herself worthy of the tales hidden within her grandmother's journal.

As the train continued, Lycian and the girl engaged in conversation, their words weaving a tapestry of shared memories and unknown adventures. They discovered common threads, moments their grandmothers had experienced together, and Lycian grinned grudgingly at her, her haughty face really bothered Lycian.

This encounter was a reminder that her journey wasn't just about her grandmother's stories.

Perhaps, in time, she would come to appreciate the presence of this girl, Betty, and the unique perspective she brought to their shared heritage.

With the train hurtling toward their destination, Lycian and Betty continued to converse, their voices blending with the rhythmic clatter of the tracks. As they delved deeper into the stories that shaped their grandmothers' lives, Lycian couldn't help but feel a sense of kinship forming—a connection forged through the intertwining narratives of their shared past.

They left the train, Betty now talking about her grandmother's art and cooking skills.

"She's amazing at cooking Ratatouille Ravioli! Oh, her art skills are so splendid. She is just so cool and finds it easy, give her a brush and with a few strokes she'll create a masterpiece." That was only one sentence of Betty's braggy behaviour, even more was added like how she was so pleasant and gave her art to people in need so they can sell it for money.

Lycian gave a reluctant smile and every conversation Betty made, Lycian would go "yeah!" or "cool!" and even "my ancestors could never!".

"Are you going to go now? I have business to attend to." Lycian said, praying for Betty and her to depart ways, trying to push the clingy girl away from her, but Betty disagreed.

"I have nowhere to go, and we are *friends* now!" Betty hopped with her and smiled.

Friends? Are you *serious?* Lycian thought, We are not *friends, Betty!* Never in a million years, *Betty.* Go away, *Betty!* Get the hell out of here.

Betty had perceived the fuming look on Lycian, and Lycian had presumed that Betty understood her fault and she started to remain calm and cool.

I guess I can tolerate this idiot for a while, let's see if she's really remorseful.

Chapter 5: The Door Of Utmost Beauty

The streets of Manchester extended before Lycian and Betty, their footsteps echoing against the pavement as they ventured deeper into the heart of the city. Tall buildings stood as silent sentinels, casting elongated shadows in the fading light of the day. The air was tinged with a vibrant energy, a harmonious blend of urban vitality and historic charm.

As they strolled along, Lycian's eyes were drawn to a narrow place slipped between two imposing structures. It beckoned to her, murmuring of hidden secrets and untold tales.

Intrigue swelled within her, and she motioned to Betty, her eyes sparkling with excitement.

"Let's explore that alleyway," Lycian suggested, her voice filled with curiosity and anticipation.

Betty's eyes widened, mirroring Lycian's enthusiasm. "I'm with you. It feels like there's something extraordinary waiting to be discovered," she replied.

They turned into the alleyway, leaving behind the bustling city streets. The sounds of cars and people faded into the background, replaced by a quiet stillness. Overgrown ivy climbed the walls, as if nature was attempting to reclaim the space. It felt as if they had stepped into a different world, a hidden realm untouched by time.

As they ventured deeper into the alley, a remarkable sight greeted their eyes—a picturesque green garden, flourishing with vibrant flowers and lush foliage. The colours danced in harmony, their fragrance hanging in the air like a sweet melody. The serenity of the garden enveloped them, offering a respite from the outside world.

But it was the sight of a wooden planked door nestled within the greenery that captivated them the most. The door stood tall and proud, its surface adorned with intricate carvings and a touch of whimsy. It exuded an aura of mystique, as if it held the key to a world of untold wonders.

Lycian and Betty exchanged glances, their hearts pounding with a shared curiosity. Without uttering a word, they understood that the door held the promise of something extraordinary—an invitation to embark on a journey beyond their wildest dreams.

Lycian and Betty stood before the wooden planked door, their hands hovering inches away from the weathered handle. It seemed to emanate a subtle warmth, as if it held the accumulated stories of generations past. The carvings etched upon its surface depicted mythical creatures, intricate patterns, and symbols that hinted at a world of wonders beyond.

A soft breeze rustled the leaves of the surrounding foliage, as if nature itself was urging them to step forward. This was a moment of choice, an opportunity to embrace the unknown and venture into the *Realm of Utmost Beauty*.

They shared a glance of unwavering resolve, Lycian and Betty grasped the handle together, their fingers intertwining. As they turned it, the door creaked open, revealing a passage bathed in a soft, ethereal light. A melodic hum filled the air, reminiscent of a distant choir, enticing them forward.

Taking a tentative step, Lycian crossed the threshold, her senses instantly overwhelmed. The world on the other side was a kaleidoscope of colours, an artist's palette bring to life.

Flowers of every imaginable hue bloomed in radiant splendour, their petals dancing in the gentle breeze. Lycian's breath caught in her throat as she marvelled at the sight, her heart swelling with awe.

Betty followed closely behind, her eyes wide with wonder. "This place... it's beyond anything I could have imagined," she whispered, her voice filled with reverence.

Lycian nodded, her gaze drifting to the horizon. Rolling hills stretched as far as the eye could see, adorned with meandering streams and majestic trees. Tranquillity enveloped them, as if the very essence of nature had embraced their presence.

As they ventured further into this mystical realm, they discovered hidden paths that led to secret gardens, each one more breath-taking than the last. Waterfalls cascaded down cliffs, their crystalline waters shimmering in the sunlight. Exotic birds flitted through the air, their melodies adding to the symphony of nature. Lycian and Betty couldn't help but feel a deep connection to this enchanted world, as if they had finally found a place where they truly belonged.

But as they delved deeper into this realm of utmost beauty, they began to sense a subtle shift in the atmosphere. A faint whisper echoed through the air, carried by the gentle breeze. It spoke of forgotten tales and ancient prophecies, hinting at a grand destiny that awaited them.

Guided by an unseen force, Lycian and Betty followed the whisper, their steps quickening with each passing moment. The path led them to a magnificent structure—an ancient, ivy-covered temple, its architecture an exquisite fusion of styles from different eras. The aura of mystery and power emanating from within was palpable.

With trepidation mingled with anticipation, they approached the temple's towering entrance. The massive doors, intricately carved and adorned with precious gemstones, stood before them like guardians of an age-old secret. Without hesitation, Lycian reached out and pushed open the doors, revealing a chamber bathed in an otherworldly glow.

Inside, they found themselves surrounded by ancient artifacts and relics, each one carrying a story untold. Symbols etched into the walls seemed to come alive, pulsating with energy. It was as if the very essence of the realm resonated within these walls, waiting for them to unlock its mysteries.

Lycian and Betty exchanged a knowing look. This was their moment—to uncover the truth, to unearth the secrets that had been dormant for centuries. They stepped forward, their hands brushing against a weathered tome.

Surrounding them was a room full of vivid murals, life and colour. Unimaginable.

Chapter 6 – Past Strikes

With each step, the soft illumination grew brighter, enveloping them in a warm embrace.

The passage seemed to stretch infinitely, an invitation to embark on a transformative journey. As they proceeded along, they noticed something glimmering in the distance.

Drawing closer, they discovered a collection of artifacts carefully displayed on pedestals, each one bearing a connection to the long-forgotten pandemic that Sally Harriet had lived through.

Among the artifacts were worn journals, reminiscent of Sally's and Alicia's own writings, filled with first-hand accounts of the struggles and triumphs of that bygone era.

Photographs captured distressing moments frozen in time, showcasing acts of resilience, compassion, and human spirit. Newspapers and documents chronicled the scientific advancements and societal changes that had shaped the course of history.

It was a poignant reminder of the collective strength and resilience of humanity in the face of adversity. They knew that these artifacts held stories that needed to be shared, to ensure that the lessons of the past were not forgotten and to inspire future generations.

Deep in thought, Lycian contemplated reaching out to an archaeologist team, maybe some sort of an organization dedicated to preserving and disseminating historical knowledge. They would provide a platform for these artifacts to be studied, analyzed, and shared with the world. It was an opportunity to shed light on the experiences and sacrifices of those who had lived through the pandemic, fostering understanding and appreciation for the human spirit.

Lycian and Betty carefully took the artifacts, capturing their significance through photographs and detailed descriptions. They knew that these tangible remnants of the past held immeasurable value, not only in preserving history but also in shaping the present and future.

As they continued their exploration of the passage, they encountered more artifacts, each one adding another layer to the story of the pandemic. They marveled at the courage and resilience of the people who had lived through those trying times, drawing strength from their shared experiences.

As the passage extended further, Lycian and Betty reached a magnificent door, bathed in a golden radiance. It stood as a symbol of enlightenment and transformation, beckoning them to step through and share their discoveries with the world.

But before they could open the door and step into the unknown, they exchanged a solemn vow. They pledged to honour the stories of the artifacts, to ensure that the lessons learned from the past would not fade into obscurity. They would reach out to the ArchaeOlogyHub, and together, they would bring the artifacts to light, preserving the wisdom of the past for generations to come.

And so, with purpose and the weight of history on their shoulders, Lycian and Betty prepared to embark on the next phase of their journey. What awaited them beyond the golden door remained a mystery but armed with the artifacts and their commitment to preserving the past, they were ready to shine a light on the echoes of the pandemic and illuminate the path to a brighter future.

As Lycian and Betty emerged from the golden door, they found themselves back in the enchanting landscapes of the realm. The weight of their discoveries and the significance of the artifacts lingered in their minds. They knew that sharing these treasures with the world was essential, but the question of how to proceed weighed heavily upon them.

Finding a peaceful spot beneath a towering oak tree, Lycian and Betty settled down to discuss their next steps. The decision to reach out to the ArchaeOlogyHub required careful consideration. They understood that sharing the artifacts would ensure their preservation and enable a wider audience to learn from the past. However, they also grappled with the desire to protect the realm's secrets and preserve its sacredness.

"I believe it is our responsibility to share these artifacts," Lycian spoke softly, her eyes reflecting a mixture of determination and reverence. "The stories they hold can inspire and educate. They can remind people of the resilience and strength that emerged from the pandemic. But we must ensure they are treated with the utmost respect and understanding. Do you know any archaeology societies that are protected and trustworthy?"

Betty nodded; her gaze fixed on the artifacts nestled safely within their satchels. " I agree, Lycian. These artifacts hold a legacy, and it is our duty to honour that legacy by sharing them.

Oh, and I know a place, Alicia's told me about it, it's called the ArchaeOlogy Hub, I believe. The ArchaeOlogyHub can provide a platform for their study and dissemination, but we must also impress upon them the importance of preserving the realm's sacredness and the lessons it holds."

Deep in contemplation, they considered the potential consequences of their decision. Would the artifacts lose their mystique and become mere relics of the past? Would the realm itself be exposed to exploitation and commercialization? These concerns lingered in their minds, prompting them to proceed with caution.

After a long discussion, Lycian and Betty reached a consensus. They would approach the ArchaeOlogyHub, but with a set of conditions. They would insist on the utmost respect for the artifacts and the realm's history. They would advocate for responsible sharing and interpretation, ensuring that the stories told would honours the individuals who had lived through the pandemic.

With their plan in place, Lycian and Betty set out on the journey back to their own world. They carried the weight of their experiences and the responsibility of sharing the realm's treasures. The road ahead would not be without challenges, but they were determined to navigate them with integrity and purpose.

Arriving at the ArchaeOlogyHub, they were greeted by a team of passionate researchers and historians. They shared their journey, unveiling the artifacts that had been carefully preserved. Lycian and Betty emphasized the importance of maintaining the realm's sacredness and the need to tell the stories with reverence and authenticity.

The ArchaeOlogyHub team listened intently, acknowledging the significance of their mission. They assured Lycian and Betty of their commitment to responsible preservation and interpretation. Together, they formed a partnership built on mutual respect and a shared goal of honouring the past while shaping a better future.

And so, the artifacts found their new home within the halls of the ArchaeOlogyHub. The stories they held were meticulously studied, catalogued, and shared with the world. Lycian and Betty's journey had sparked a renewed interest in the realm's history and the lessons it held for humanity.

As for Lycian and Betty themselves, their adventure had left an indelible mark on their lives. They became advocates for preserving the realm's sacredness and the importance of learning from the past. Their journey had forged a deep friendship, and together, they continued to explore new avenues of knowledge and understanding.

And as the realm's stories echoed through time, Lycian and Betty's decision to share the artifacts became a testament to the power of history, the resilience of the human spirit.

The artifacts unveiled at the ArchaeOlogyHub served as a reminder of the strength and resilience displayed by individuals during the pandemic. They bore witness to acts of bravery, compassion, and unity that had emerged amidst adversity.

The stories contained within those artifacts captivated the hearts and minds of people from all walks of life. They became a source of inspiration, encouraging individuals to face their own challenges with courage and determination. The artifacts became a testament to the indomitable spirit of humanity, reminding people that even in the darkest of times, hope and resilience can prevail.

Lycian and Betty, fuelled by their experience in the realm, became advocates for resilience and the power of storytelling. They embarked on a mission to share the lessons learned from the pandemic, not only through the artifacts but also through their own voices.

They travelled to schools, universities, and community centres, captivating audiences with their tales of adventure and discovery. They spoke of the realm's hidden garden, the golden door, and the artifacts that held the stories of a generation. Their words inspired others to delve into their own histories, to uncover the stories that had shaped them, and to find strength in the collective human experience.

The impact of Lycian and Betty's journey reached far and wide. Their efforts led to the creation of a global network of storytellers and historians dedicated to preserving and sharing the narratives of resilience. Through exhibitions, workshops, and digital platforms, they created spaces where people could come together to learn, connect, and find solace in the shared human experience.

The ArchaeOlogyHub, guided by Lycian and Betty's vision, became a beacon of knowledge and understanding. It continued to curate and showcase artifacts, ensuring that the stories they held would never be forgotten. Researchers, historians, and visitors from around the world flocked to the hub, seeking to deepen their understanding of the past and draw strength from the lessons it offered.

In the years that followed, Lycian and Betty's partnership flourished. They published books, collaborated on documentaries, and engaged in conversations that explored the resilience of the human spirit. Their work became a catalyst for positive change, encouraging individuals and communities to reflect on their own experiences, acknowledge their struggles, and embrace the resilience that resides within them.

And as the realm's artifacts continued to inspire generations, Lycian and Betty realized that their journey had only just begun. There were countless stories waiting to be discovered, lessons waiting to be learned, and individuals waiting to be empowered. They knew that their role as custodians of resilience was one that would endure, igniting a spark of hope and resilience in the hearts of all those they encountered.

And so, armed with the stories of the past, Lycian and Betty ventured forth into a world hungry for inspiration and strength. They would continue to share the tales of the realm, of the golden door, and of the artifacts that had unlocked the power of resilience within them.

As they embarked on their next adventure, their hearts filled with purpose and their spirits ablaze, Lycian and Betty knew that the journey to resilience was not just a solitary path—it was a collective endeavour, woven together by the threads of shared stories.

Arinel had also reached out to the Hub and found out about Lycian's whereabouts, it was a heart-touching instant, as mother and daughter completely met after years of pausing and misery, Arinel couldn't be furious, she should've been gratified for Lycian's exploratory habits, even Caspian teared up and hugged his sister.

Chapter 7 – The Train Of Departure is here! Tickets, Please!

Time had passed since Lycian and Betty first embarked on their remarkable journey, Lycian had actually grown. Their bond had grown deep, and they had become inseparable companions, united by their shared experiences and a passion for uncovering the hidden stories of resilience. But as with all paths in life, theirs eventually reached a crossroad.

Lycian and Betty found themselves standing at the edge of a sun-kissed meadow, a serene backdrop for their final moments together. The gentle breeze whispered through the grass, as if bidding farewell to a chapter that had been written with fervour and determination.

"I cannot express how grateful I am for this incredible journey," Lycian spoke, her voice laced with joy. "We have seen and experienced things that will forever shape us. The memories we've created will forever be etched in my heart."

Betty nodded, her eyes shimmering with a mix of gratitude and a tinge of sadness. "Lycian, you have been the truest friend I could have asked for. Our shared passion for uncovering the stories of resilience has taken us to places beyond our wildest dreams. I am forever grateful for the moments we've shared and the strength we've drawn from one another."

As they gazed at the vast expanse before them, a sense of understanding passed between them. They knew that their paths had diverged, leading them to separate destinations that awaited their individual journeys.

"It's time for us to embark on our own paths," Lycian said softly, a bittersweet smile gracing her lips. "There are stories yet untold, and new adventures awaiting us. But know that you will always hold a special place in my heart, Betty. Our paths may separate, but the bond we've forged will endure."

Betty returned the smile, her eyes reflecting both acceptance and a glimmer of excitement.

"Lycian, you are a true force of resilience, and I have no doubt that you will continue to inspire and touch lives wherever your path takes you. Remember, our journey together has prepared us for whatever lies ahead. Farewell, dear friend."

With a final embrace and a shared moment of unspoken gratitude, Lycian and Betty began their respective journeys. Each step they took led them toward new adventures, challenges, and the opportunity to continue sharing the stories of resilience that had ignited their spirits.

As the sun dipped below the horizon, casting a warm glow upon the meadow, Lycian and Betty took their first steps, their hearts filled with a profound sense of gratitude and a renewed commitment to embrace the paths that awaited them.

And so, they parted ways, their spirits intertwined in the tapestry of resilience, forever connected by the memories they had created and the strength they had found in one another.

As Lycian ventured forth into the unknown, she carried within her the stories of the realm, the wisdom she had gained, and the unwavering belief in the power of resilience. With each new chapter written, she would continue to honours the legacy they had uncovered and inspire others to embrace their own journeys of resilience.

And as Betty embarked on her own path, she held close to her heart the shared moments of discovery and the unbreakable bond she had formed with Lycian. She would carry their shared stories with reverence, ensuring that the lessons of resilience would continue to touch the lives of those she encountered.

Their individual paths would weave through the tapestry of time, branching out to touch the lives of countless others. And though they had departed ways, their spirits remained forever connected, their journeys a testament to the enduring power of resilience and the profound impact that friendship and shared purpose can have on our lives.

Lycian journeyed onward, she found herself immersed in new landscapes, encountering diverse cultures, and unearthing stories of resilience in every corner of the world. She became a beacon of hope and inspiration, using her own experiences and the tales she had discovered to empower others to embrace their own resilience.

Through her captivating storytelling and unwavering determination, Lycian touched the hearts of many. She became a sought-after speaker, sharing her insights and lessons at international conferences and events dedicated to the celebration of the human spirit. Her words resonated deeply, reminding people of their inherent strength and their capacity to overcome even the most formidable challenges.

Meanwhile, Betty found her own path in the world of academia. Driven by her passion for history and the stories of resilience she had encountered alongside Lycian, she dedicated herself to scholarly research. Betty's expertise and knowledge grew, and she became a renowned historian, sought after for her expertise in uncovering and preserving forgotten narratives.

Their paths continued to intersect, albeit in different ways. Lycian would occasionally invite Betty to join her on special projects, where they would combine their unique talents to shed light on stories that had yet to be told. Their collaborations were cherished moments of reunion, as they celebrated their shared purpose and the profound impact they had made on each other's lives.

As the years went by, Lycian and Betty continued to grow individually, drawing strength from the journeys they had undertaken. They remained close friends, supporting each other from afar, celebrating each other's accomplishments, and offering a listening ear during moments of doubt or challenge.

And though their paths had taken them on separate adventures, the bond forged in their shared pursuit of resilience remained unbreakable. They understood that their connection transcended physical distance and time, and that their friendship would forever serve as a reminder of the transformative power of resilience and the profound impact we can have on each other's lives.

In the twilight of their own journeys, Lycian and Betty found solace in the knowledge that their pursuit of resilience had made a difference in the lives of many. The stories they had unearthed, the lessons they had shared, and the inspiration they had ignited had created a ripple effect, touching countless souls and sparking a collective awakening to the indomitable human spirit.

As they reflected upon their shared adventures and the paths they had chosen, Lycian and Betty embraced the truth that their journey together had been an extraordinary gift—a testament to the power of resilience, friendship, and the unwavering belief in the ability of every individual to rise above adversity.

And so, as their individual journeys drew to a close, Lycian and Betty found solace in the knowledge that their paths had intertwined for a reason. They had enriched each other's lives, leaving an indelible mark on their hearts and a legacy of resilience that would continue to inspire generations to come.

As they bid each other farewell once more, their spirits soared with gratitude for the transformative journey they had shared. They understood that while their individual stories would continue to unfold, their bond would forever serve as a testament to the enduring power of resilience, friendship, and the unwavering belief that within each of us lies the strength to overcome, the courage to persevere, and the capacity to inspire others along the way.

And so, as Lycian and Betty embraced their separate destinies, they carried with them the memories of their shared adventures, the lessons of resilience, and the unbreakable bond that would forever tether their spirits together. With hearts full of gratitude and souls brimming with the wisdom they had gained, they stepped into the final chapters of their respective journeys, ready to embrace the unknown with a renewed sense of purpose and a steadfast belief in the resilience of the human spirit.

Glossary

From Chapter 1 – 3

Plumose: Having feather-like or feathery characteristics.

Inane: Silly, lacking sense or meaning.

Frolicking: Playing or moving about cheerfully and energetically.

Crossly: In an annoyed or irritated manner.

Insolent: Showing a rude and arrogant lack of respect.

Rubicund: Red or reddish in complexion.

Repute: The opinion or estimation in which someone is generally held; reputation.

Lurid: Vivid in a shocking or sensational way.

Cerulean: Deep blue in colour.

Impulsive: Acting or done without forethought.

From Chapter 4 - 7

Refectory: A dining hall or room, especially in a religious institution or college.

Sanatorium: A medical facility for long-term treatment or recuperation, often used for patients with chronic illnesses.

Death-bell disease: A fictional disease mentioned in the story.

Mind reader: Someone who has the ability to read or perceive the thoughts of others.

Apocalypse: A widespread and usually catastrophic event that results in the collapse of society or a significant disruption of normal life.

From Chapter 8 – End Of Story

Antidote: A substance that can counteract the effects of a poison or toxin.

Perseverance: The quality of continuing to work hard and not giving up even in the face of difficulties or obstacles.

Amity: A friendly and harmonious relationship or atmosphere.

Venerosis: A fictional rare and deadly disease caused by a toxin found in the Veneroi plant.

Resilience: The ability to recover quickly from difficulties or hardships.

About the Author Page

Name: Iba Malik

Biography:

Iba Malik is an 11-year-old talented young writer with a boundless imagination. From a young age, Iba discovered her love for storytelling and has since captivated readers with her vibrant imagination and relatable characters.

Writing Style:

Iba's writing style is characterized by its whimsical adventures, relatable characters, and vibrant imagination. Her stories are filled with joy, friendship, and valuable life lessons that resonate with readers of all ages. Despite her young age, Iba possesses a remarkable ability to capture the essence of childhood and convey it through her storytelling.

Literary Achievements:

While Iba is still at the beginning of her literary journey, her friends and family are her biggest fans, eagerly awaiting each new tale she spins. Her ability to transport readers to imaginative worlds and her knack for creating relatable characters have already made an impact on those who have read her stories.

Influences:

Iba finds inspiration in the world around her. She is deeply influenced by classic authors such as Jamila Gavin and J.K. Rowling, whose imaginative worlds have sparked her own creativity. Iba's own experiences and the everyday wonders of life also serve as a wellspring of inspiration for her storytelling.

Writing Process:

Iba's writing process is a joyful exploration of her imagination. She allows her ideas to flow freely, often discovering the magic within her stories as she writes. Iba embraces feedback from her family and teachers, continuously honing her craft and improving her storytelling skills.

Future Projects:

The future holds endless possibilities for Iba's writing journey. She is excited about the prospect of expanding her storytelling beyond short stories and dreams of writing her first full-length novel. Iba also hopes to connect with other young writers, collaborating on creative projects and exchanging ideas. With her talent and passion for storytelling, Iba's future projects are sure to captivate.

Don't miss out!

Visit the website below and you can sign up to receive emails whenever Iba Malik publishes a new book. There's no charge and no obligation.

https://books2read.com/r/B-A-PTNW-BQWHC

BOOKS 2 READ

Connecting independent readers to independent writers.

About the Author

I am a talented young writer who, at 11 years old, wrote this book. As a dedicated writer, I have always been passionate about the power of words to convey emotion and ignite the imagination. I draw inspiration from my own life experiences, and this book is no exception. Dedicated to my dad, I have poured my heart into this work, creating a literary masterpiece that will resonate with readers of all ages. Despite my young age, I have already established myself as a gifted writer with a writing style that is both engaging and thought-provoking. My passion for writing shines through on every page of this book, and readers will surely be captivated by my unique voice and compelling storytelling.